DYLAN'S AMAZING DINOSAURS

THE TYRANNOSAURUS REX

For Xander and Lily, with love x—E.H.

For George Bear, my wonderful nephew—D.T.

First edition for the United States, its territories and dependencies, and Canada published in 2015 by Barron's Educational Series, Inc.

First published in Great Britain in 2014 by Simon and Schuster U.K. Ltd., London

Text © copyright 2014 by E.T. Harper
Illustrations © copyright 2014 by Dan Taylor
Paper engineering by Maggie Bateson
Paper engineering © copyright 2014 by Simon and Schuster U.K.

The right of E.T. Harper and Dan Taylor to be identified as the author and illustrator of this work, respectively, has been asserted by them in accordance with the Copyright, Designs, and Patents Act, 1988.

All inquiries should be addressed to:
Barron's Educational Series, Inc.
250 Wireless Boulevard
Hauppauge, NY 11788
www.barronseduc.com

ISBN: 978-1-4380-0643-7

Library of Congress Control Number: 2014942966

Date of Manufacture: December 2014
Manufactured by: Leo Paper Products Ltd., Kowloon Bay, Hong Kong, China

Product conforms to all applicable ASTM F-963 and all applicable CPSC and CPSIA 2008 standards. No lead or phthalate hazard.

Printed in China
9 8 7 6 5 4 3 2 1

DYLAN'S AMAZING DINOSAURS

THE TYRANNOSAURUS REX

E.T. HARPER AND DAN TAYLOR

BARRON'S

Dylan had an amazing tree house. It was full of fantastic things, and the most fantastic of all were Grandpa Fossil's magic Dinosaur Journal and . . .

Keep Out!

WINGS, Dylan's toy pterodactyl!
He came to life whenever Dylan opened the journal,
and they flew off on great adventures together to
make awesome dinosaur discoveries.

"Hey, Wings!" Dylan called as he flung the journal open.
"I wonder what discovery we'll make today?"

Fact File

Bite: Three times as strong as a great white shark

Size: 40 feet (12 m)—as long as a bus and the weight of two elephants

Habitat: Forests, plains, and swamps

Extraordinary feature: Teeth the size of a man's hand

Number of teeth:..........

Tyrannosaurus rex
↓

"Hmm..." Dylan said. "So that's our mission, Wings!
We need to find out how many teeth the T. rex had!"

At the mention of a Dino Mission, Wings came to life,
shook out his wings, and swooped down from the shelf.

"Let's go, let's soar, off to the land
where the dinosaurs roar!" Dylan shouted.

Dylan grabbed his binoculars as they flew over Roar Island.

"Look, Wings! A hadrosaur, a stegosaurus, a triceratops, and there's a TYRANNOSAURUS!"

"Quick, let's land before we lose it!"

Dylan hopped off Wings, and inched forward to get
a better look at the gigantic creature. But he got too close . . .

ROOOAAAARRRRGGHHHHH!

The T. rex caught Dylan's scent in its nostrils. It turned its giant head, and bared its GINORMOUS teeth.

"Yikes!" cried Dylan as he started to run. "Are those teeth for real?"

The ground shook beneath his feet. "Fly over the T. rex Wings!" shouted Dylan. "We have to confuse it."

Dylan ran as fast as he could, but the T. rex was still gaining.

Dylan dived, out of breath, into a hollow log. "Phew, that was close!"

The T. rex stopped. And sniffed.

The ferocious beast opened its jaws so wide that Dylan could feel its disgusting breath on his face.

Dylan needed a plan, and fast!

"Got it!" he said and crawled to the other end of the log.

"Time to go!"

Dylan ran out of the log just as the
Tyrannosaurus sank its teeth in.

The giant dino shook its head and growled in frustration.
Dylan's plan had worked—the T. rex's teeth were stuck! Dylan
dived into a nearby swamp and watched the T. rex try to get
its teeth out of the log.

Finally, with an earth-shaking snarl, the T. rex freed its fearsome fangs. Turning its head, it hunted for its Dylan-shaped dinner.

Sinking lower into the swamp, Dylan disguised his scent with stinky mud, pulled grass over his head, and hid. He held his breath as the Tyrannosaur's beady eyes and supersensitive nose moved over him.

It felt like forever, but at last the T. rex caught sight of
a tastier-looking dinosaur dinner and charged off.

Dylan searched the sky for Wings. "Help!
The T. rex has gone ... but now I'm really sinking!"

Just in time, Wings swooped down and pulled Dylan out.

"Wow! Thanks, Wings!" called Dylan. "Now, let's get that missing information before the T. rex comes back for dessert!"

Wings dropped Dylan by the log.
"Its teeth are HUGE!" said Dylan as he started to count the holes.

"One, two, three . . .
          fifty-six, fifty-seven . . .

                    FIFTY-EIGHT TEETH!
                              That T. rex has the meanest bite EVER!"

"Dino Mission accomplished, Wings! Let's fly!"

Dylan jumped on the pterodactyl's back, and they took off for home.

Back in the tree house, Dylan grabbed an apple and took a huge bite, lifting the magic Dinosaur Journal onto his lap.

He scribbled the number 58 into the T. rex fact file.

G. FOSSIL

"Hey Wings, look!" Dylan held out his apple.
"I can count my teeth, too!"

Smiling, Wings folded up his wings and jumped back onto
the tree house shelf, ready and waiting for their next adventure.

LOOK OUT FOR MORE AMAZING ADVENTURES
WITH DYLAN AND WINGS!

OUT NOW—

THE STEGOSAURUS